12 DAYS OF CHRISTMAS

12 DAYS OF CHRISTMAS

RACHEL ISADORA

G. P. PUTNAM'S SONS • AN IMPRINT OF PENGUIN GROUP (USA) INC.

REBUS KEY

1 partridge in a pear tree

2 turtledoves

3 French hens

4 calling birds

5 gold rings

6 geese a-laying

 **7** swans a-swimming

 **8** maids a-milking

 **9** ladies dancing

 **10** lords a-leaping

 **11** pipers piping

 **12** drummers drumming

On the first day
of Christmas,
My true love gave to me
A partridge in a pear tree.

On the second day
of Christmas,
My true love gave to me
2 TURTLEDOVES
and a

On the third day
of Christmas,
My true love gave to me
3 FRENCH HENS

and a

On the fourth day of Christmas,
My true love gave to me

4 CALLING BIRDS

  and a

On the fifth day
of Christmas,
My true love gave to me
5 GOLD RINGS

and a

On the sixth day of Christmas,
My true love gave to me
6 GEESE A-LAYING

and a

On the seventh day of Christmas,
My true love gave to me
7 SWANS A-SWIMMING

and a

On the eighth day of Christmas,
My true love gave to me
8 MAIDS A-MILKING

  and a

On the ninth day of Christmas,
My true love gave to me
9 LADIES DANCING

   and a

On the tenth day of Christmas,
My true love gave to me
10 LORDS A-LEAPING

 5 4 3  2 **and a** 1

On the eleventh day of Christmas,
My true love gave to me
11 PiPERS PiPiNG

    **and a**

On the twelfth day of Christmas,
My true love gave to me
12 DRUMMERS DRUMMING

7 6 5 4 3 2 and a 1

MAP OF AFRICA

MALI

GHANA

NIGERIA

SWAZILAND

SOUTH AFRICA

I spent a great deal of time in Africa and learned about its people and their way of life. I saw people carrying chickens on their heads, living in round houses called rondavels and performing on stilts.

The "lords a-leaping" pay tribute to dancers from Mali. The "ladies dancing" were inspired by women from Swaziland. The "drummers drumming" show drums played in Ghana and Nigeria. The woman wearing "five gold rings" was modeled after women in South Africa.

Through the illustrations in this book, I hope to share with you my wonderful experiences in Africa.

—RACHEL ISADORA

For Elizabeth and Richard

G. P. PUTNAM'S SONS

A division of Penguin Young Readers Group. Published by The Penguin Group.

Penguin Group (USA) Inc., 375 Hudson Street, New York, NY 10014, U.S.A.

Penguin Group (Canada), 90 Eglinton Avenue East, Suite 700, Toronto, Ontario M4P 2Y3, Canada (a division of Pearson Penguin Canada Inc.).

Penguin Books Ltd, 80 Strand, London WC2R 0RL, England.

Penguin Ireland, 25 St. Stephen's Green, Dublin 2, Ireland (a division of Penguin Books Ltd.).

Penguin Group (Australia), 250 Camberwell Road, Camberwell, Victoria 3124, Australia (a division of Pearson Australia Group Pty Ltd).

Penguin Books India Pvt Ltd, 11 Community Centre, Panchsheel Park, New Delhi – 110 017, India.

Penguin Group (NZ), 67 Apollo Drive, Rosedale, North Shore 0632, New Zealand (a division of Pearson New Zealand Ltd).

Penguin Books (South Africa) (Pty) Ltd, 24 Sturdee Avenue, Rosebank, Johannesburg 2196, South Africa.

Penguin Books Ltd, Registered Offices: 80 Strand, London WC2R 0RL, England.

Published simultaneously in Canada. Manufactured in China by South China Printing Co. Ltd.

Design by Marikka Tamura. Text set in Geist.

The illustrations were done with oil paints, printed paper and palette paper.

Library of Congress Cataloging-in-Publication Data

Isadora, Rachel. 12 days of Christmas / Rachel Isadora. p. cm.

Summary: Resets the traditional Christmas carol in Africa, using a combination of text and rebuses. Includes author's note about some of the African traditions depicted.

1. Folk songs, English—Texts. 2. Christmas music—Texts. [1. Folk songs—England. 2. Christmas music. 3. Carols. 4. Africa—Fiction. 5. Counting. 6. Rebuses.]

I. Twelve days of Christmas (English folk song) II. Title. III. Title: Twelve days of Christmas. PZ8.3.I76Aaf 2010 782.42—dc22 [E] 2009052862

ISBN 978-0-399-25073-6

1 3 5 7 9 10 8 6 4 2